# Snug

# Michael Morpurgo

## Snug

With illustrations by
Faye Hanson

Barrington Stoke

First published in 2013 in Great Britain by
Barrington Stoke Ltd
18 Walker Street, Edinburgh, EH3 7LP

www.barringtonstoke.co.uk

Text © 1974 Michael Morpurgo
Illustrations © Faye Hanson

ISBN: 978-1-78112-286-0

Printed in China by Leo

This book has dyslexia friendly features

*To Ella, Lottie and Charlie*

# Contents

# Chapter 1
# Snug the Kitten

Snug was my sister Lisa's cat. No one ever gave Lisa the cat – they just grew up together. I don't really remember Lisa being born, but it seems that Snug turned up a few weeks before she did. Dad found him wandering about, crying and mewing.

It was after a cat shoot in the barns. The farm workers shot the stray cats once in a while because they breed so fast.

Dad found Snug crying round the barn door. His mother must have been killed, or maybe she had run off.

Anyway, Dad picked Snug up and brought him home.  He was so young that his eyes weren't open yet.  Mum had to feed him warm milk with an eye dropper.

By the time Lisa was born Snug was
a healthy kitten. Lisa used to cry a lot –
it's the first thing I remember about her.
Come to think of it, she still howls more
than she should. Snug took to curling
up under her cot when she was inside,
and beside her pram if she was sleeping
outside.

## Chapter 2
## A Pair

I first remember noticing that Lisa and Snug were a pair when Lisa was learning to walk. One day she was staggering about the kitchen doing a record-breaking run from the sink to the kitchen table – all five feet of it. Snug padded up to her and gently nudged her off balance into the dog bowl.

The bowl was full of water.  We all fell about laughing while Lisa sat there and howled.

Snug adored Lisa and followed her everywhere. He'd go on walks with her, just as long as she left the dog at home.

Lisa used to bury her face in his fur and kiss him as if he was a doll, but he loved it and stretched himself out on his back for his tummy to be tickled. Then he'd purr like a lion and shoot his claws in and out in bliss.

## Chapter 3
## Snug Grows Up

Snug grew into a huge cat. I suppose you would call him a tabby cat. He had grey and dusty-white stripes with a smudge of ginger on his soft belly. He had great pointed ears, which he flicked and twitched even when he was asleep.

He came in every evening for his food, but he never really needed it, or if he did he certainly never showed it.

He didn't often get into fights, and when he did, they hardly ever left a mark on him. He was either a coward or a champ.

He'd come in in the morning, after a night's hunting, full of mice and moles and voles, and lie down on Lisa's bed.

He'd purr himself to sleep and wake up just in time for his evening meal, which Lisa served him at five each evening.

No one ever got angry with Snug. Everyone who came to the house would admire him as he stalked through the long grass, or sunbathed by the vegetable patch. Lisa would preen herself whenever anyone spoke about him.

Lisa could never understand why Snug killed birds. In the early summer he used to tease two or three baby thrushes or blackbirds to death a day. Lisa very nearly went off him at this time every year.

One time he found a robin's nest at the bottom of a hedge – he'd been drawn to it by the cheeps.

By the time we got there, he'd scooped out three baby robins and there were several speckled eggs lying broken and scattered on the ground. Lisa didn't speak to him for a week, and I had to feed him.

But they made it up, they always did.

# Chapter 4
## Scrapes

Now and again Snug wandered off into the barns and fields to look for a she-cat to visit. This must have taken a long time, because he disappeared sometimes for 24 hours or so – but never longer, except once.

Mum and Dad were home and Snug was late coming in. We'd had our bath and were sitting watching telly. 'Tom and Jerry' I think it was, because it was our favourite DVD and we always put it on before we went to bed.

There was a yowl outside the kitchen door, more like a dog in pain than a cat. Lisa disappeared into the kitchen and I followed. I'd seen 'Tom and Jerry' a hundred times before anyway.

Lisa opened the door and Snug came in, worming his way round the doorway. His head hung down and his tail was drooping, not held up straight like normal. One ear was covered in blood and there was a great scratch across his face. He'd been in a fight and he was badly hurt.

Lisa picked him up gently and put him in his basket.

"Get the cotton wool and some water ... and hurry!" she said.

Snug lay there panting while Lisa cleaned up his wounds.  I handed over cotton wool and salt water and then clean water when Lisa had finished with that.

Lisa must have spent an hour or more nursing that cat, and all the time I didn't say a word to her. I knew she'd cry if I talked to her.

Mum came in after a bit to wash up. She bent over the basket.

"He'll be all right, dear," she said.
"It's not as bad as it looks.  You'll see,
he'll be right as rain by the morning.
Why don't you see if he'll take some
warm milk?"

Lisa nodded. I knew she wouldn't heat the milk herself, because then she'd have to turn round. She hated to let anyone see her face when she was upset. I put the milk on the stove and Mum cleared up.

Lisa put a saucer of milk down by the basket and Snug went to it almost straight away.

He crouched over the milk and drank slowly, his pink tongue shooting in and out.

What happened next, happened so suddenly that none of us had time to react.

Mum bent down to put some potato peel in the bin. Then she lifted the bin and opened the door to empty it. In a flash, Snug was out the door. We just stood there, the three of us. Mum clutched her bin, I held the milk pan and Lisa rubbed her eyes, all red with crying.

Lisa rushed after Snug, calling into the night. We all tried. Even Dad came away from the telly and called. But Snug would not come.

## Chapter 5
# Worry

We tried to tell Lisa that Snug would be all right.  Dad put his arm round her and stroked her hair before we went up to bed.

"If he'd really been ill, love, he wouldn't have taken any milk," he told her.

He was a great dad sometimes. "He'll be back tomorrow, you'll see," he said.

We went off to school as normal the next morning. No one even said Snug's name at breakfast.

Most days we walked along the road to school to meet up with our friend Tom, but this morning Lisa wanted to go through the fields.

We left the house early and went off past the farm buildings where Snug used to hunt. Lisa searched round the tractor sheds and calf pens, while I clambered over the straw in the Dutch barn.

It was no good – there wasn't enough time.  We had to get to school.

"It'll be all right, Lisa," I said.  "Don't worry."  It was the best I could do.

School went on and on that day.
Lisa was even quieter than normal.  She
spent playtime looking over the fence
into the orchard behind the playground.

In our lessons she kept looking out of the window, and I could see her getting more and more worried.

Lunch came and went, and it started to rain.  By the time we were let out, it was pouring down.  Lisa grabbed her coat and rushed out.

There was still no sign of Snug at home. We searched and called until it was dark and Mum came home from work. The time for his meal passed – still no Snug.

Dad came home a little later than normal. We were in the front room, Lisa and I, and we heard him talking in a low voice to Mum in the kitchen.

We were mucking about trying to mend my train set on the floor when Dad came in.

He didn't flop down in his armchair but stood there all tall and near the ceiling.  He hadn't taken his coat off.  It was dripping on the carpet.

"Lisa," he said. "I'm sorry, love, but we've found Snug. He's been killed. Run over. Tom's father found him down by the main road. It must have been quick, he wouldn't have felt anything. I'm sorry, love."

Lisa turned away.

"Are you sure it's him?" I said. "There's lots of cats like him about."

Lisa ran out of the room and upstairs, and Mum went up after her.

"It's him all right," Dad said. "I've got him in the shed outside. I thought we'd bury him tomorrow, if Lisa wants us to." Dad sat down. "It's him all right, poor old thing."

## Chapter 6
# Broken

"Can I have a look at him, Dad, just to be sure?" I said.

I didn't feel like crying. Somehow I couldn't feel sad enough. I was interested more than upset. It was strange because I really liked that cat.

Dad took me over to the shed and switched on the light.  There he was, all stretched out in a huge cardboard box. He didn't even cover the bottom of it.

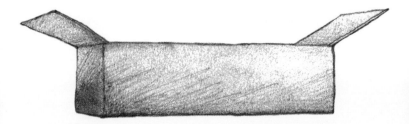

His fur was matted and soaked.
There was no blood or anything – he just
lay there all still, with his eyes closed.

"Well?" Dad mumbled behind me.
"It's him, isn't it?"

It was him all right, the same ginger tummy, and the same tabby markings. He didn't look quite so big lying in that box.

"He's so still, Dad," I said. "Why isn't he all broken up after being run over? You'd think he'd be squashed or something."

"When you lift him, he doesn't feel right, but I expect he was thrown clear on impact," Dad said. "Go on now, you'd better go and see Lisa."

When I got up to my bedroom, Mum was in with Lisa and I could hear a lot of crying. I hate that – I never know what to say to people when they're like that. I went and lay on my bed and tried to feel sadder than I really was.

I was more sorry about Lisa than old Snug. He'd had a fairly good run, after all. Lots of food and love and a cosy place to sleep. What more could a cat want?

And for some reason I got to thinking of a party the mice would be holding in the Dutch barn that night to mark Snug's death.

# Chapter 7
# At the Door

I was down early in the morning before anyone else. I'd forgotten to feed the goldfish the night before. I was dropping the food in the tank when I heard Snug's voice outside the kitchen door.

There was no mistake.  It was his usual 'purrrrrp ... p ... p' – a sort of demand for someone to open the door right away.

I wasn't hearing things. I opened
the door and in Snug came, snaking his
way round the doorpost, as happy and
contented with himself as ever.

I screamed upstairs, "He's here!  He's back!  Snug's back!"

Well, of course, they didn't take long to get downstairs, and Lisa was weeping all over him and looking him over as if she couldn't believe it.

Dad and I buried the other cat after breakfast. We dug a hole in the woods on the other side of the stream and wrapped him in one of Dad's old gardening jackets.

When we got back, I saw Dawnie from school in the garden with Lisa.

Mum met us by the gate. "It was Dawn's cat," she said. "It's been missing for a couple of days and it looks just like Snug. Dawn wants to see where you've buried it."

We took Dawnie across the stream and into the woods.

As we walked back home I was glad that Snug hadn't died. I thought about how the mice wouldn't be having their party in the Dutch barn, after all.

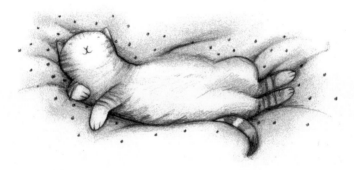

Our books are tested
for children and young people by
children and young people.

Thanks to everyone who consulted on
a manuscript for their time and effort in
helping us to make our books better
for our readers.

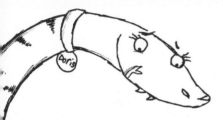

Have you read
the other
Little Gems?

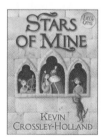